For Noah
Don't grow up too
fast!

Pat A. Mar

Poems to grow by

Patricia A. Maurice

ISBN 978-1-61684-079-1
Poems to grow by
Copyright © 2020 Patricia A. Maurice
All rights reserved
First edition

I've been writing these poems since I was just a child. I dedicate them to the child within all of us.
--Patricia Maurice 2020

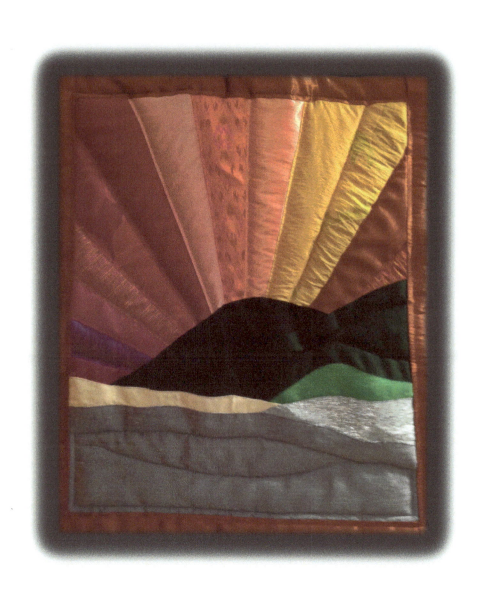

Poems and Pages

I. Ever a Child

Lorelei	8
China doll	9
The tin soldier	10
Wussie Winkie	12
Too small	14
The dollhouse	16
The land of the Jub Jub Jo	17
Hum like a hummingbird	18
Mama deer	19
88 keys	20

II. Near and Far

Don't ever	22
Grandma remembers	23
Who's cat	24
Happy Dog	25
Eating 'round the world	26
The drifting sand	28
Grandpa's hammer	29
Visiting Grandma	30
Visiting Grandpa	31
Hopsy bunny	32
Backyard adventures	33
The Highlands	34

III. Nature's Mystery

Enchanted seeds	36
Magical mystery	38
The whole hole	39
The nanometer	41
Oil and water	43
Envioussssss	44
Arachnid dreams	45
The sand grain	46

IV. The Rhyme's the Thing

Otta otter	50
Word slips	51
The rude poem	52
The scary poem	53
Rhyming fool	54
Brain dust	55
Dino games	56
ABC	58

V. Wise and Foolish Poems

Too many words	60
Stars to dust	61
Hamlet's pals	62
Polonius' last act	63
Wise old rhymes	64
Tools for life	65
Factory or farm	66
The simple path	67
Oh little bird	68
Freedom	69

Part I
Ever a Child

Lorelei

The sun was shining brightly on little Lorelei.

She came running, almost dancing, with a twinkle in her eyes.

A basket full of flowers swung on her arm so fair

And a pretty yellow ribbon was tied up in her hair.

Where have you been? I scolded, you've worn my patience thin.

She looked up with her big brown eyes and broke into a grin.

Why Uncle, she chided, to put me in my place,

I picked some golden daisies for Auntie's favorite vase.

I couldn't help but chuckle at this most delightful sight

So she seized two fingers of my hand and led in graceful flight.

As we strolled across my grounds, her curls played with the breeze.

Dancing merrily to the tune she sang with perfect ease.

China doll

China doll, china doll, what a pretty friend you'd be.
China doll, my china doll, awake and speak to me.
China doll, china doll, sing out just like a bird.
But china doll, my china doll, will never speak a word.
China doll, china doll, what a pretty friend you'd be.
China doll, my china doll, awake and speak to me.
China doll, china doll, be live for just one day.
But china doll, my china doll, must just spin on her way.
China doll, china doll, what a pretty friend you'd be.
China doll, my china doll, awake and speak to me.

The tin soldier

One little tin soldier, that's all that I see.
But that little tin soldier means so much to me.
His shoulders are broad and his head is held high.
His eyes don't look down; they gaze at the sky.
Short crimson jacket, pants colored gray.
A perfect lieutenant in every way.
One little tin soldier, that's all that I see.
But that little tin solder means so much to me.
Every night while I am in bed
He marches around with his hat on his head
But ev'ry morning at the break of day
He's standing so still in the same old way.
One little tin soldier, that's all that I see.
But that little tin soldier means so much to me.

I wish I could stay up all through the night
Marching beside him in silver moonlight.
We would be bravest of brothers and kin,
One made of flesh and the other of tin.
One little tin soldier, that's all that I see.
But that little tin soldier means so much to me.
Of glory in battlefields far, far away
I dream with my soldier ev'ry day.
But know in my heart 'twould be braver still
To march for peace over valley and hill.
One little tin soldier, that's all that I see.
But that little tin soldier means so much to me.

Wussie Winkie

Wee Wussie Winkie's a saucy little sprite
Who lives behind my ear and tells me stories day and night.
Sometimes he is so jolly playing bells that ring-a-ling
I run around in circles shouting choo-choo as he sings.
But, when at night my mama says it's time for me to bed
That naughty little prankster runs around my head
And mixes up my brain by prancing all about
Til all that I can do is scream and kick and shout.
Silly little Wussie hangs beneath my nose
Sticking out his tongue and tickling with his toes.
He runs across my tummy and rolls across my chest
Then dives into my belly-button as a jest.

Oh, what trouble Wussie makes with all the tricks he plays

Til mama teases Wussie so he finally runs away.

Then crying turns to laughter and then to drooping eyes.

While mama tucks me into bed with kisses and sweet sighs.

Oh Wussie, give me happy dreams and whisper in my ear

The peaceful, loving thoughts that good boys and girls should hear.

For soon I will grow older and my wussing spells will end.

But mama will remind me I once had a saucy friend.

Too small

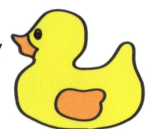

Other kids have normal names
Like Ai, Jamir, or Paul
But mine seems kinda weird
Because it's just 'TOOSMALL.'
When I try to reach a glass
From a kitchen cabinet
I need a step stool 'cause
I'm just TOOSMALL for it.
When I want to buy ice cream
The countertop's too high
I'm just TOOSMALL to see
Which kind I want to try.
I've learned not to ask for
A roller-coaster ride.
Other kids can have fun
I'm TOOSMALL for the guide.
I'd like to try ping pong
Bowling or basketball.
Why ask if I can play
They'll say I'm just TOOSMALL?
I'm just TOOSMALL for clothes
That at my age seem fine.
I'll still wear chicks and ducks
When I am ninety-nine!

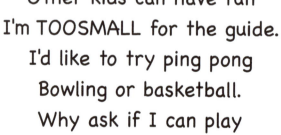
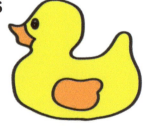

My mom and dad tell me
Don't do that, you're TOOSMALL.
You'll drop it, you'll break it
You'll trip, you'll slip, you'll fall!
But...
My feet are not too small
To run and dance and skip.
My hands are small enough
To fit where yours can't slip.
I don't eat half as much
Or outgrow my new shoes.
Old ladies think I'm smart,
Old men just get confused.
Small packages are good.
The hobbits are the best.
Thank God for little things
That we have all been blessed.
I really do not care
If I stay just the same,
Besides, to tell the truth
I've grown to like my name.

The dollhouse

When you are just a tiny girl
Who needs to escape the too big world
Without a room to call your own
Or rooftop where you can be alone
Then you're the luckiest girl of all
If you've a house made for your dolls.
Could my Daddy somehow see
When he built a dollhouse for me,
In his heart, did he know...
That I would need a place to go
Where I could have a quiet mind
And leave the busy world behind?
My dollhouse has always been
A land where I can just imagine
Anyone, any thing, any place
Far beyond the miniature space.
It's where my mind is free to roam
It's where I feel most at home.

The land of the Jub Jub Jo

Under the tiddley-widdley bridge in the land
of the Jub Jub Jo
There is a place where the sun shines bright
And the cold winds never blow.
Where children play all through the day
And think it un-tellably neat
To stuff themselves on pudge-pudge pie
That's always warm and sweet.
Even at school, there's hardly a rule
And never a care nor a fright,
For a smile well turned is a lesson learned
And ever a popular sight.
In the cold December when you're tired and tempered
And bored 'cause there's no place to go,
Just close your eyes and sail with surprise
To the land of the Jub Jub Jo.

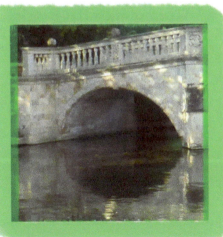

Hum like a hummingbird

Hum like a hummingbird.
Croak just like a frog.
Stand for one second
Silent as the fog.
Pop up like a dandelion
Looking to the sun
Spin like a spider
When her web is done.
Hop like a bunny rabbit
Then just like a toad.
Roll like a wheel
But not on the road!
Be a falling snowflake
Imagine if you can
How it would feel to
Melt like a snowman.
Fold like an umbrella
Dance like the rain
Bow your head in prayer
Then do it all again.

Mama deer

Mama dear, mama deer,
Do you have a baby near?
A sweet spotted little fawn
To sleep beside you dusk to dawn.

Mama do not let your baby
Grow too fast or run too wild.
For God loves best the little ones
Your wee fawn and my wee child.

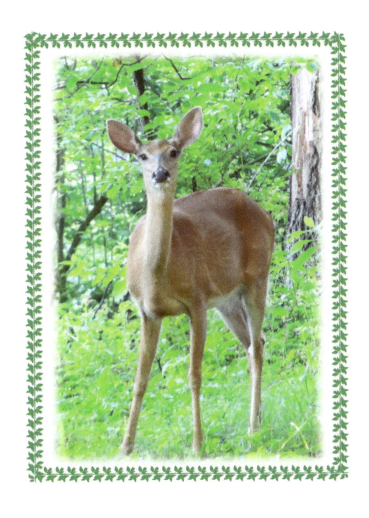

88 keys

Eighty-eight keys lined up together
Dressed in your finest black and white
I can make friends out of foes
If I can learn to treat you right.

Eighty-eight keys, somber and secret
Like oracles in a trance
Then I start to tease you and
You all begin to sing and dance.

Eighty-eight keys, working together
Form melodies out of my poems
Even when my fingers slip, you
Still bring magic to my home.

Eighty-eight keys, playing together
Can make a perfect harmony
But it takes practice to perfect
All of you and all of me.

Eighty-eight keys, lined up together
Now you must be very brave
Because my small hands never will
Stretch across a full octave.

Part II
Near and Far

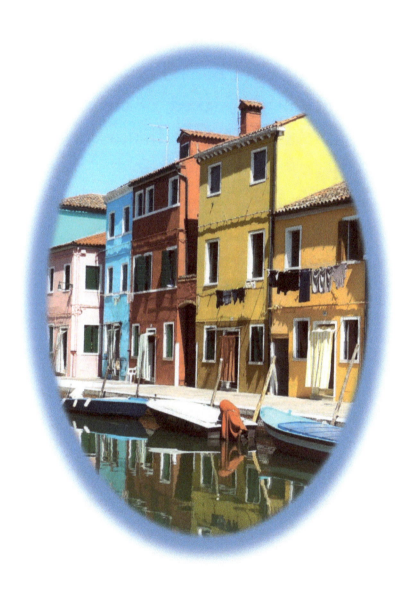

Don't ever

Don't ever tickle a dinosaur
Don't wrestle with a porcupine
Don't try to tell a lion
Your roar's not as loud as mine.
Don't walk behind a horse
You will get kicked, of course.
Don't fish with too thin a line
You know it will break, every time.
Don't sneak up on a sleeping skunk
Or pillow fight on a bunk.
Don't make a mess with your junk
Or I will lock it in a trunk.
Don't try to steal, for goodness sake,
A rattle from a rattlesnake.
Many things you learn in school
But listen to the golden rule:
Never talk to Dad before he's had
His first coffee of the day.
This one rule you MUST obey.

Grandma remembers

Did you know there was a time
When if you wanted to make a rhyme
You couldn't look one up online
It had to come from your own mind?

If you wanted to go and meet
A friend on some unknown street
You couldn't find it with one tap
You had to learn to read a map.

If you played a capital game
And you didn't know a name
You had to ask Grandpa to pass
An old book he called Atlas.

It's hard to believe, but I've sworn
Your mother actually wasn't born
With a cell phone in her hand
I know, it's hard to understand.

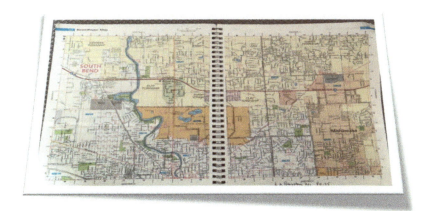

Who's cat?

Did you ever have a cat?
And did that cat grow very fat?
Did you feed him eggs and ham
And on Thanksgiving candied yam?
Did you scratch him 'til he'd purr
Then thank you with a ball of fur?
Did he sit in your best chair
And leave it covered with his hair?
Did you ever wonder if
Your cat would kick you off a cliff
Any time he felt like it
Then wave good-bye with hiss and spit?
Cats are cats and that is true
They only do what they will do.
And since you are so stubborn too,
Tell me, child, whose cat are you?

Happy Dog

Happy Happy Happy Dog
Happy Dog
Happy Dog
Happy Happy Happy Dog
Happy Happy
Dog
Happy Happy Happy Dog
Dog Dog
Dog
Happy Happy Happy Dog
Dog
Happy
Dog

Eating 'round the world

I've traveled all round the world sampling many
a tasty dish
Fresh-cooked couscous, hot tamales,
lingonberries, gefilte fish,
Red bean cakes, warm chapatis, apple bananas,
apfelstreudel,
Polish kielbasa, Swiss raclette, currywurst, hot
Pho noodle,
Veggie tagine, Greek baklava, brats and fries,
fish 'n chips,
Shrimp salad in avocado, shiro wat, sriracha dip,
Belgian waffles, chocolate sauce, strawberries
and cream,
Turkish delight, gerkhin pickles, Kalua pork,
seafood steam,
Paella colored gold with saffron, soup stained
red from beets...

Spotted dog, haggis, sausage, then for dessert yum yum treats.
Butterscotches, pomegranate, grits, fried okra, shoofly pie.
Once I tried a Bangkok curry so spicy hot it made me cry.
I've eaten with just my hands, with chopsticks, or a plastic spoon,
By gripping tidbits with injera, under sun, rain, or moon.
Not all spice was to my liking, not everything I'd try again
But, eating all these different foods, along the way, I made new friends.

The drifting sand

Drift sand drift.
Blow wind blow.
Sit a little while with me
Until it's time to go.

The wind will blow
You far across the sea.
And you will drift
Far away from me.

I loved you before
You were born.
I've washed each stitch
Of clothes you've worn.

I've held your hand
And watched you fall.
And treasured
Each moment, all.

Every child
Is meant to grow
And it becomes
Your job to go.

But even though
You must depart,
You'll always be
My child, my heart.

Grandpa's hammer

This is your Grandpa's hammer.
I wonder if you knew
He used it his whole life long.
Now it belongs to you.
He built our family's house
From foundation to slate.
Grandpa could build anything
Right and true, strong and straight.
I hope that you will use it
As often as you may.
If you wield it like Grandpa
You'll never go astray.

Visiting Grandma

Oh how I love my Grandma so.
Though her hair is white as the snow
She plays hide and seek with me.
And helps me climb her apple tree.
She taught me to quilt and fish.
And showed me how to make a wish
On the first star I spy
Peeking through the evening sky.
Grandma's house smells so nice
Like warm bread and cinnamon spice.
She doesn't care what mess I make
When she teaches me to bake.
Mom says Grandma spoils me rotten
But, Mom, if you've forgotten
How important it is to be
Youthful, curious, and carefree
Don't worry, because we two,
Gran and I, can both teach you.

Visiting Grandpa

My Grandpa takes me for a walk
So we can have a real guy's talk.
He tells Grandma that when we're out
We're always sure to talk about
Things that help me grow up smart
Like science, music, math, and art.
But Grandma probably has guessed
That we discuss what guys like best.
She probably thinks that we ponder
Cars and computer games when we wander.
Do you think it would break her heart
To know we mostly talk of

Football
Airplanes
Reptiles
Trains and
Spiders?

Hopsy bunny

Big bunny little bunny,
Hop hop hop.
If I could be a bunny rabbit
I would never stop.
I'd hop out to the garden
To find a breakfast treat.
Then hop down the driveway
To see whom I might meet.
I'd hop by the mailbox
I'd hop through the gate.
I'd hop to get ice cream
Wouldn't that be great?
I'd hop past a green house
I'd hop past the blue.
But when the sun was setting
I'd hop back home to you.

Backyard adventures

You can spend your life traveling
Earth's every corner near and far.
But in the end, you'll never find
More magic than in your back yard.

The Highlands

Have you heard the mountains singing?
Do the bagpipes call your name?
Does the river laugh to greet you?
Will you bow then do the same?

Does the heather's rustic beauty
Free the essence of your soul?
Does the trail forever beckon?
Do the Highlands make you whole?

Part III
Nature's Mystery

Enchanted seeds

When I first hung a box of seeds outside my windowsill,
I never could have dreamt of all the joy it would instill.
First, with his cap of black, as bold as visitor could be
Came swooping in with nimble flight a jolly chickadee.
A titmouse followed close behind, now searching all around
Looking ever curious with her tussled, tufted crown.
A sparrow brown like winter trees--which type I wouldn't guess
Til she turned round and I could glimpse the 'stickpin' on her breast.
One afternoon, a flight of golden finches came along
All gibbering and wrestling, at least a dozen strong.
More gaudy still, some reddish cousins joined the growing fun,
Though I admit their feathers looked near purple in the sun......

Woodpecker--Red-capped, zebra striped you pulled a short-lived coup
But, you'd be far more stately if your belly weren't red too.
So many cardinals gathered round that I could scarcely hope
That in another day or two they'd crown a feathered pope.
While a host of slate-gray juncos foraged wide upon the ground,
Some silly mister nuthatch ate his dinner upside down!
A cup of seeds and dried out corn a pauper's price to pay
To conjure magic from the skies, whisk loneliness away.
Each one that journeys near or far some precious time to spend
Somehow, I cannot help but think of you as lifelong friend.

Magical mystery

There's a magical stuff on Earth
Its formula is H_2O.
It fills up rivers, lakes and seas
And even makes up ice and snow.
It's hidden deep beneath the ground
Though we can sometimes pump it up
And, use it in our factories
Or drink it from a glass or cup.
Too little and we have a drought,
Too much turns into raging flood.
It's in the vegetables we grow
And even makes up most of blood.
It can be fresh and tasty cool
Or as salty as the deepest sea.
For some it costs a mound of gold,
For others, it is always free.
It's the reason why Planet Earth
Looks blue as blue from outer space.
I love it in the morning when
As dew it drops down on my face.
You and I are mostly made up
Of this mystery magic stuff.
And if you want to guess its name
I think I've said more than enough.

The whole hole

I
Found
a hole in
my backyard
and though it looked quite
small, I poked it with a twig
and found it wasn't quite so small at all.
I thought, perhaps the hole was dug out by
a tiny vole, or maybe engineered by a tunneling mole.
Suddenly, a tug pulled the twig out of my hand...
There must be something bigger beneath my land!
I used a stick expecting to pry out a fat chipmunk.
But, the stick was yanked from my hand; it made a thunk!
Could this hole be the warren of some enterprising rabbit?

I tried a bigger stick but, whoosh, something grabbed it.
I cut an old branch off a tree and with a little jog
  Rammed the branch
    straight down the hole,
      expecting a ground hog.
        But, I never met a ground hog yet
          that was so quick a snatcher.
            Ah, certainly the hole must belong
              to a mighty badger!
                I cut a sapling and poked it
                  into the badger's sett.
                    But, it got swallowed up so fast,
                      the critter must be bigger yet!...

Could it be a den of wolves or of a burly big black bear?
Surely I could find a tree large enough to stick in there.
In went a tree, and with a start I suddenly began to think
I should take more care because the hole began to sink.
And a sink hole is something that might just swallow me.
So maybe I should leave the hole alone, don't you agree?
The moral of this story is absolutely clear:
Never be so cavalier
to judge the whole
from whatever
small hole
that may
at first
to you
A
P
P
E
A
R

The nanometer

I have a little friend who is small as small can be
In fact, she's about a billion times smaller than me.
For such a tiny gal, she has the most protracted name.
She's called Nanometer, but I love her just the same.
I cannot see her even with the best light microscope
If she weren't so clever, I don't know how I would cope.
Her behavior is a mystery, often I can't tell
What she will do next, though I believe I know her well.
No matter how long I wait, she will never settle down.
Her physics are so complicated, they make me frown.
Ms. Nanometer, you are frustrating as can be.
Ah, but you're a magician when it comes to chemistry!

Oil and water

Did you know that oil and water
Never, ever like to play?
When water flows in his direction,
Oil turns fast and floats away.
Whenever oil is poured on water,
Oil curls up into a ball
And they both strive to keep
Their contact area oh so small.
But little soap is such a darling,
Sparkling like an uncut gem
She refuses any prejudice
And is friends with both of them.
She politely asks of water
If she might hold his hand
Then does the same with oil,
And, even though it wasn't planned...
Soon the three of them are dancing
All together, side, by side
For water becomes less haughty
As soon as oil's emulsified.

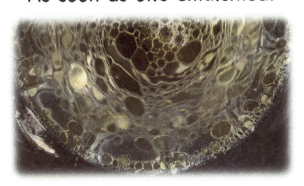

Enviousssss

Why are princes always frogs?
Why can't they be snakes?
Snakes are such handsome fellows.
Oh, for goodness sake.
I've eaten so many froggy
Princes that here's the thing...
Skip the whole snake prince idea
And just make snakes kings.

Arachnid dreams

I'm just a little spider
Don't squash me
Pretty, pretty please.
If you do, I promise you
I'll come back
And haunt you
In your dreams.
I can almost
Hear the screams!

The sand grain

Magic little grain of sand
Are you from a foreign land?
Did you blow across the sea
To spend a moment here with me?
Were you once a mountain high
Towering so close to the sky?
Did you laugh at a small cloud
Were you then so very proud?
Did you bounce along a bank
Of some river, 'til you shrank
From a boulder to a cobble
Then a pebble, just a bauble?

Did you meet a dinosaur
On some mid-Jurassic shore?
Did Eophis one time slip
Or Eohippus perhaps trip
Over you, so smooth and round
Lying still, upon the ground?
Did you roll into the sea
Into a trench, deep buried
Slowly turned into a melt
Along some ancient mountain belt
A big volcano belched and then
You became a rock again?

After millennia came and went,
Was a man one day sent
To place you somewhere high amid
Some obelisk or pyramid?
Since human works do not last long
Did you join a sandy throng
Atop some hot Sahara Dune
Blown by wind beneath the moon
Across the Earth transported far
All the way to my back yard?
Shiny little grain of sand,
Sitting so still in my hand,
What mysteries could be told
By the magic that you hold?
What great adventure will unfold
Long after I have turned to mold?

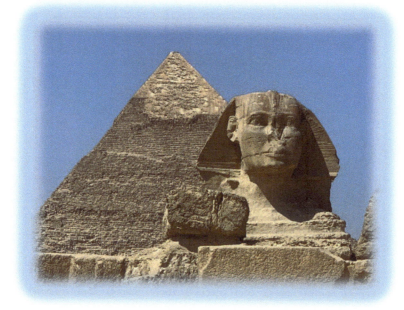

Part IV
The Rhyme's the Thing

Otta Otter

Do you think an otter wonders what an otter ought to do?

Do you think a big fish fishes for a little fish or two?

Do you think a deer is just as dear as cuckoo is cuckoo?

Do you think a fly can fly all day then the whole nighttime through?

If a duck ducks beneath a duck, can a goose goose a goose too?

Do you think a whale lets out a wail whenever she feels blue?

Do you think a kid can kid a kid like I am kidding you?

Word slips

A word tripped across my tongue and landed on my lip.
The next in line laughed so hard that she began to slip.
All their little wordy friends thought that it looked like fun
So they tripped and slipped and got stuck, too, every one.
Soon my mouth was so full from the silly wordy game
That try as I might, I could not even say my name.
The words squirmed and tickled me and caused a sneeze,
AH-CHOO!
Then they all came tumbling out and made this poem for you.

The rude poem

Well, if my rhyme made you smile,
Even just a little while,
I hope you will think it fair,
If I sit down in your chair,
And try a sip of your tea
Then nibble your last cookie.
Can I steal your slippers too?
Not the polite thing to do.
But I need them now to roam
All around your cozy home.
Are your toes as cold as ice?
That must not feel very nice.
Sorry... but Oh me, Oh my
So much better you than I.
I supposed you might conclude
That this poem is rather rude.
If you think that, then my friend...
Time for me to rudely end.

The scary poem

Well, did you ever know a poem
That somehow snuck inside your home,
And when it was time for your bed
Crawled in your ear and round your head?
Perhaps repeating wussie rhymes
Over and over many times.
A poem like that can cause a fright
That it could stay there through the night.
And still it might not go away
When you wake up on the next day.
Such scary poems, to me, it seems,
Should only come at Halloween.
But...
Ask any poet, they will say
It's hard to make a poem obey.
Don't worry, it will be okay.

Rhyming fool

Did you ever make a rhyme?
Oh yes, I do it all the time.
Before I'm out of my bed
A rhyme will pop into my head.
If I let it freely roam
It often will become a poem.
If I do not catch it quick,
It might become a limerick.
Though I'm sure I never knew
Of any that became Haiku.
If it's in me all day long,
It sometimes turns into a song.
If you stick around here, you'll
Begin to call me rhyming fool.
If you do not run away,
I might make you a rhyme someday.

Brain dust

OOH
I love a house full of dust
And a garden full of weeds
Off
To my garden we will dash
To plant some dandelion seeds
We
Can have such fun sprinkling
Fairy dust around my home.
Then
We'll check the coop to see
If the chickens need more bones
While
We're at it, we can deliver
Pails of milk to calves and cows
But
I think the sheep have all been
Fleeced more than enough for now
Perhaps
I could try to brain you
Although it might be rather tough
If
You've figured out this riddle
Your head's already full enough.

Dino games

Why can't a dinosaur have a nicer name?
With a better name, they'd still be just the same.
A name that is shorter, easier to spell.
That doesn't need a Ph.D. to pronounce well.
Allosaurus, Brachiosaurus, Camarasaurus aren't that bad.
But trying to say *Dromiceiomimus* just makes me mad.
Who ever thought *Eustreptospondylus* was a good idea?
And, surely *Fukiuraptor* is not a name meant to endear.
Ok, *Gigantosaurus* does sound kind of cool.
But poor *Heterodontosaurus* was probably teased in school.
Can you imagine what *Irritator*'s mom used to say to him?
Don't you think that *Juravenator* could just have been Jim?

Kritosaurus, Lapparentosaurus, Muttaburrasaurus
Nemegtosaurus, Opisthocoelicaudia, Pachycephalosaurus.
Quaesitosaurus, Rebbachisaurus... just ignore us.
Thank goodness for my old friend *Tyrannosaurus Rex*.
Just shorten it to *T. Rex* and it's definitely the best.
The dinosaur alphabet keeps getting worse by far
Though I admit *Velociraptor* could be a sports car.
Why didn't anyone give a dinosaur a name
That would make it easier to play a dino game?
A sweet name like flower, a short name like Thor
OMG, I can't believe they named one *BAMBIRAPTOR*!

ABC

Did you ever see the sea
Waving with a wave?
Could it be
That a bee
Always behaves?
I do not think
I ever knew
A new gnu.
How 'bout you?
If you can
And I can
Then I guess
We toucan
Someday dance
The Can Can?

Go and sit
By the sea.
You be A
I'll be B
Together, we'll be

Part V
Wise and Foolish Poems

Too many words

Is it a toad or just a frog?
Is it a swamp or a small bog?
Is it a race where we all win?
Or is it the name you call my skin?
Is it an alligator or crocodile?
Bahr al Ghazal, Iteru, or Nile?
Is it McKinley that stands so high?
The great one, Denali so near the sky.
Is it a word or is it a name?
Are we all different or just the same?

Stars to dust

When stars shine down on us
They really do not care
The color of our faces
How curly is our hair.
The sun shines just as brightly
If we are short or tall
Though we should not cast shadows
On those who are too small.
God hears us no matter
Which languages we speak
We all turn to dust someday
Despite the gold we seek.

Hamlet's pals

We two lie without our heads
With a graveyard for our beds
In a strange and foreign land,
Buried deep beneath the sand.

We have no mouths, we have no eyes.
We have no brains to make us wise.
What, find our heads now that they're gone?
We used them not when they were on!

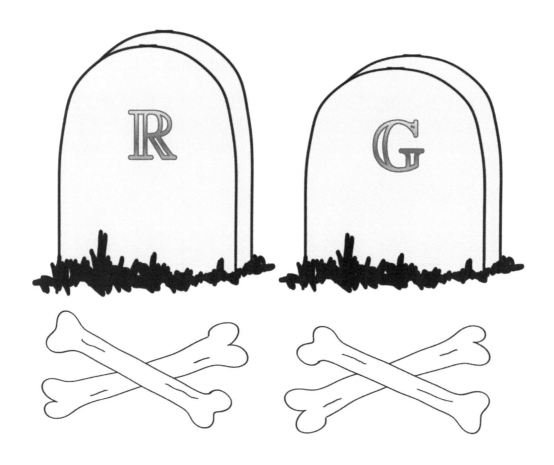

Polonius' last act

I was a fox.
A fox was I
The counselor to the king.
And as a fox
I was a spy.
I knew most everything.
I had a son.
A daughter too.
I taught them both the truth.
Not by my actions
But my words.
I was so sly forsooth.
But then one day
A fine young man
Filleted me like a cod.
I knocked at heaven
But, by Jove,
I couldn't outfox God!

Wise old rhymes

Anything you ever buy
You will have to cook or clean
So I hope you always try
To live your life lean and green.

I believe there are few things dumber
Than refusing to call a plumber.

A cake may have no nose or eyes
But it will always find your thighs.

If you have to wash the dishes
Despite your prayers and wishes,
You will have far less troubles
If you learn to love the bubbles.

Tools for life

It's not always what you know
Or where you choose to go
You can be the world's worst fool
If you don't have the right tool.

Make tools for your toolbox
Out of all your missteps
If you're anything like me,
At least you'll grow strong biceps.

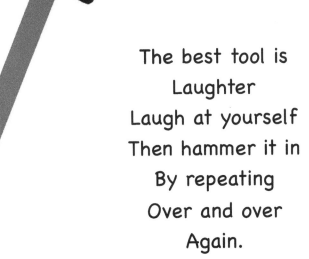

The best tool is
Laughter
Laugh at yourself
Then hammer it in
By repeating
Over and over
Again.

Factory or farm

If you want to eat good food
That brings you health, never harm
Ask whether food on your plate
Comes from factory or farm.
Food should be fresh, colorful
Natural and always pure.
It should never be too sweet
Nor too salty, that's for sure.
What to eat and what to leave
Isn't all that hard to tell.
If it came straight from a farm
It will help you grow up well.

The simple path

I'd rather chase a butterfly
Than chase a bag of gold.
I'd rather watch the green grass grow
Than worry til I'm old.
I'd rather hear a robin sing
Above its woven nest
Than dine on sparkling silverware
When simple fare is best.
I'd rather dance and sing a song
Beneath the azure sky
Than fill my head with greed and pride
And let life pass me by.
I wonder what the world would be
If every child once trod
A path through forest, field, and stream
The surest path to God.

Oh little bird

Oh little bird, oh little bird
Perched high up in a tree
I don't think I have ever heard
A song so sweet to me.
Oh little bird, oh little bird
You shine bright as the sun.
God's gifts you bring each song you sing
Perfection, every one.
Oh little bird, oh little bird
Too soon you'll fly away.
Through winter's cold, I'll be alone
'Til you return someday.

Freedom

I hope that you will someday find
The one thing that will set you free
I can't know what it is for you
But I know what freedom is for me.

To me, freedom is a walk
A walk, to me, can be as sweet
Whether it's to a mountain top
Or down a busy city street.

I have traveled my whole life
And there are places I have been
Where you can't take a walk if you're a girl
Or have 'the wrong' color skin.

Many have walked for freedom
And others have barred their way
But, in the end freedom wins
And, it always will, I pray.

Find your freedom
Wherever and whatever it may be
Until you do, perhaps you will
Walk a little while with me.

About the Author

Patricia A. Maurice is a retired professor of Environmental Geology at the University of Notre Dame. She spent many years traveling, writing, and teaching about the environment. She loves to hike, quilt, and cook for her family. Over the course of writing these poems, she grew from a small child into a mother and even a *Professor emeritus*. She's still trying to decide what she wants to do when she grows up.

A few words about the poems

I've been writing poetry since I was 8 years old, and the verses have been running around in my head; most never written down until now. Here are some of their stories:

- *Lorelei, China doll* and *The tin soldier* were all written to music when I was around 10 years old, as part of a children's ballet. *Lorelei* and *China doll* were both inspired by a ballerina music box and porcelain dolls from my grandmothers.
- *The tin soldier* was of course inspired by Robert Lewis Stevenson's classic poetry in *A Child's Garden of Verses*.
- I wrote *The land of the Jub Jub Jo* in college, when a school with no rules seemed like a great idea.
- *Wussie Winkie* was written when our son was 2-3 years old, as a ruse to stop temper tantrums. If we could get him laughing long enough to get a little orange juice in him, the temper tantrum would disappear. Then, he'd be ready to nap.
- *Too small* was inspired by the title of a book I wrote and illustrated in about third grade. It's basically the story of my life.
- My dad Robert Maurice made me a dollhouse when I was a little girl. I have continued to 'play' with it my whole life.
- *88 keys* refers to how I set my poetry to music when I was a child. I still have to stretch hard to reach an octave.
- *Eating 'round the world* started to take shape during a hiking trip in Morocco but it continues to evolve. Poems have a way of doing that.
- The first verse *of The drifting sand* was written in college, but I've re-written the rest of the poem many times throughout my life.
- *Grandpa's hammer* was written after we lost both our fathers in the same year. They were both handy with a hammer!
- I love hiking and *The Highlands* have spectacular trails.
- *Enchanted seeds* came out of the coronavirus pandemic of 2020 when bird watching was a perfect activity.
- I've spent my career studying water, so it's always on my mind. I wrote *Magical mystery* after a trip to Iceland to visit my college roommate several years ago. Water in its various forms is on full display in that magnificent country.
- My yard is FULL of holes and critters of all shapes and sizes; hence *The whole hole*.
- I'm perhaps best known as a scientist for my work on nanoparticles, which is where *The nanometer* comes from.

- I wrote a textbook on environmental surface chemistry, which explains the *Oil and water* poem. I highly recommend oil/water/soap experiments for kids of all ages!
- *The sand grain* and *Dino games* reflect my life as a geologist.
- *Otta otter* was written after a trip to Alaska. I love otters!
- Our family has a tradition of Beekeeping, *ABC*.
- *Too many words* was written during a cruise down the River Nile on a traditional felucca sailing vessel. Time slows down, and you can actually think.
- The two poems based on *Hamlet* (*Hamlet's pals* and *Polonius' last act*) were written when I was a senior in high school. I wrote an anthology of eulogies in place of an essay. And, I actually got away with it.
- *Factory or farm* was inspired by the question my husband would ask the kids whenever they sat down to eat. It's a great simple guide for kids to identify healthy foods (it works!).
- *Oh little bird* is a children's version of *Amazing Grace*.
- *The simple path* was written during a 200 mile solo hike along the Wild Atlantic Way in Ireland. Four of my great grandparents were from Ireland, and it is a land of great beauty, poetry, and countless blessings.
- I wish I could remember where all the other poems came from. They've just been rattling around my brain for various amounts of time. Some were made up for babysitting gigs. Many were edited from earlier versions because not all my poetry rhymes. A few were written just for this book. The rest….?
- I've probably used a few words (like chide, sett, iteru, and injera) that will be new to some readers. Rather than defining them, I'll let you go on a voyage of discovery to look them up.
- My family and friends, especially my mom Helen, her dear college friend my 'Aunt Connie' and our daughter Candice all provided suggestions and edits. But, I'm as willful as a cat so the errors and silliness are all mine.
- Be careful, because, to paraphrase Lee Hazlewood: This brain was made for rhymin'. That's what it's gonna do. One of these days, this brain is gonna rhyme all over you.

The photos

Locations of the photos, taken by the author:
- Front cover: Kerry, Ireland
- Inside title page: Our farm in Michigan, USA
- Dedication page: County Wicklow, Ireland
- Back of dedication page: Quilt made from silk scraps from Thailand
- Ever a child: Kerry, Ireland
- Page 11: Bourtzi Castle, Napflio, Greece
- Page 16: The dollhouse my father Robert Maurice made me ~ 55 years ago
- Page 17: Pie baked in Michigan, Bridge in Cambridge UK, Gnome from Switzerland
- Page 19: In our yard in Michigan, USA
- Page 20: The piano from my dollhouse
- Near and Far: The Venetian island of Burano
- Page 23: Map of the South Bend/Notre Dame area, Indiana, USA
- Page 24: Essaouira, Morocco
- Page 25: Monsieur Colter le Chien, High Falls, New York, USA
- Page 26: Tagine cooking in Morocco
- Page 27: My son eating with Injera at an Ethiopian restaurant in Boulder, Colorado USA; Sushi etc. in Japan; Fruit in Morocco
- Page 28: The strand, Malahide, Ireland
- Page 29: My father-in-law's hammer, Ohio, USA
- Page 30: Quilt designed and made by the author
- Pages 32 and 33: Michigan, USA (coconut shell from Hawaii, USA)
- Page 34: The Scottish Highlands
- Nature's Mystery: Rocky Mountain National Park, Colorado, USA
- Pages 36 & 37: Michigan, USA
- Page 38: leftmost photo, French Polynesia; other photos from Iceland
- Page 43: Oil, soap, and water, my kitchen in Michigan, USA
- Page 44: Michigan, USA

- Page 45: Monteverde National Park, Costa Rica
- Page 46: The author as a young paleontologist, Wyoming USA
- Page 47: Arenal Volcano, Costa Rica
- Page 48: Egypt
- The Rhyme's the Thing: Tōshō-gū shrine, Japan
- Page 50: Alaska, USA
- Page 51: Michigan, USA
- Page 53: A carnival mask brought back from Burano, Venice, Italy
- Page 56: A flake of *Camarasaurus* fossil brought back from Como Bluff, Wyoming, from the author's work with paleontologist Robert Bakker (see his book, *The Dinosaur Heresies*)
- Page 57: Michigan, USA
- Wise and Foolish Poems: Boot Lake, Elkhart, Indiana
- Page 60: Taken while floating down the Nile, Egypt.
- Page 61: Taken while hiking in the Atlas Mountains, Morocco
- Page 66: A strawberry farm in Northern Indiana, USA
- Page 67: Taken while hiking with my good friend Carole in Wales
- Page 68: Michigan,, USA
- Page 69 Hiking in Alaska, USA
- About the Author: Sweden
- This page: Colorado, USA
- Back cover: Japan